5 5 5 6 6 6 7 7 7

5 11 11 12 12 12

11 16 12

15 15 16 16 16

15 16 15

15 19 19 20

19 19 20 20

Beginner Books, Random House,
and the Random House colophon are registered trademarks
of Penguin Random House LLC.
The Cat in the Hat logo ® and © Dr. Seuss Enterprises, L.P. 1957,
renewed 1986. All rights reserved.

Visit us on the Web!
Seussville.com
rhcbooks.com

Educators and librarians, for a variety of teaching tools, visit us at
RHTeachersLibrarians.com

Library of Congress Cataloging-in-Publication Data
is available upon request.
ISBN 978-0-525-64605-1 (trade) — ISBN 978-0-525-64606-8 (lib.bdg.)

Printed in the United States of America
10 9 8 7 6 5
First Edition

Dr. Seuss's

1 2 3

Beginner Books®
A Division of Random House

1
One

One, one.
It all starts with one.
One cat on a ball
having fun.

2
Two

Two, two.
Next comes two.
Two orange antlers on
Foo-Foo the Snoo.

3
Three

Three, three.
Count to three.
Three birds sitting
in a puffy pink tree.

4 Four

Four, four.
Can you spot four?
Four friends walking
to a big pink door.

5
Five

Five, five.
Do you see five?
Five funny fish
are out for a drive.

6 Six

Look up and down.
Look side to side.
Can you count six
mouths open wide?

7
Seven

This man here
is Mr. Gump.
Mr. Gump has a
seven hump Wump.

8
Eight

Now it's time
to count to eight.
Eight weary elephants
and a tree of great weight.

9
Nine

Nine sad turtles,
each on another's back,
piled up together
in a nine-turtle stack.

10
Ten

Count ten birds.
That's what you should do.
Count ten birds
in yellow and blue.

11
Eleven

Look at his fingers!

One, two, three, four,
five, six, seven,
eight, nine, ten—yikes!
He has eleven!

12
Twelve

Can you count twelve
Curious Crandalls?
They sleepwalk on hills
with assorted-sized candles.

13
Thirteen

Count thirteen trapeezers
of the Zoom-a-Zoop Troupe.
They grab on to each other
as they zoop and they swoop.

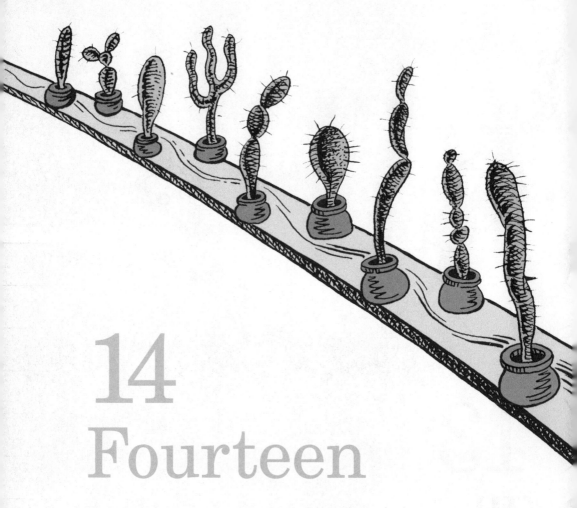

14
Fourteen

Old Mr. Sneelock
on his Roller-Skate-Skis
slides past fourteen pots
full of Stickle-Bush Trees.

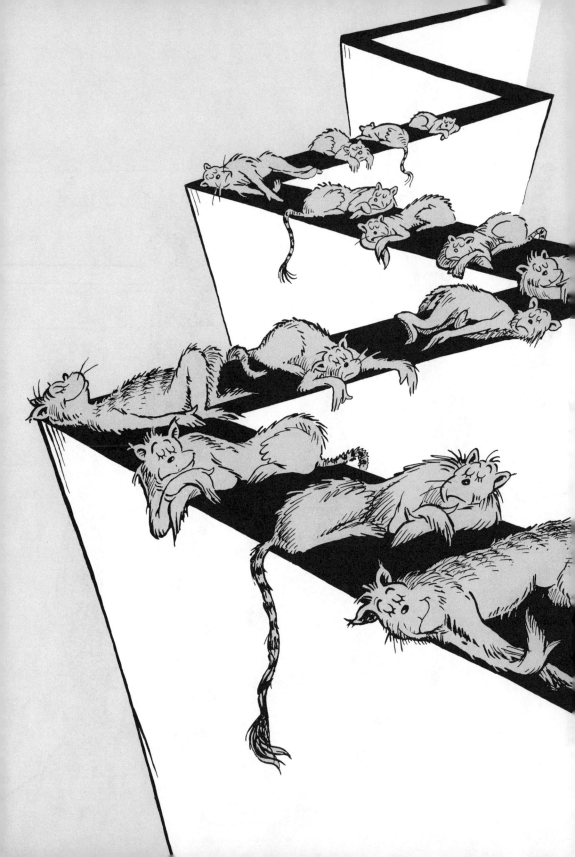

15
Fifteen

Count them. Count them.
Count them all.
Fifteen cats sleeping
on a ziggy-zaggy wall.

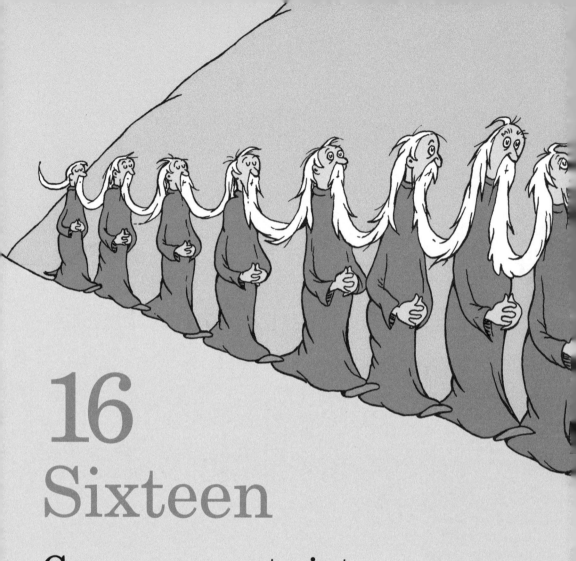

16
Sixteen

Can you count sixteen
of the Brothers Ba-zoo?
They are known far and wide
for the way their hair grew.

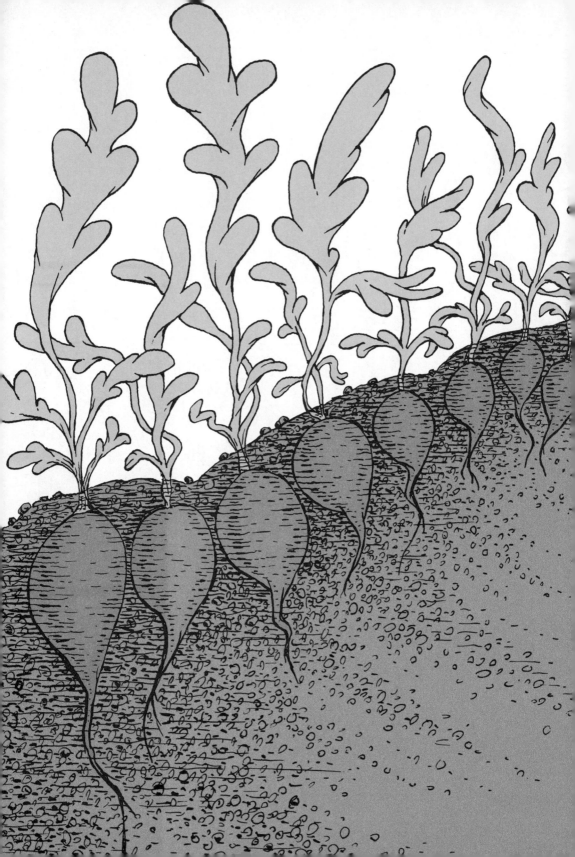

17
Seventeen

And speaking of counting,
you should be quite glad-ish
that you're not this farmer's
seventeenth radish.

18
Eighteen

Count eighteen Jogg-oons
from far desert dunes
who like to croon tunes
about pebbles and prunes.

19
Nineteen

Over the water
and into the sky,
can you count nineteen
bloogs blowing by?

20
Twenty

Start at the bottom.
Work up to the top.
Count twenty Fuddnuddlers.
(And now you can stop.)

1 1 1 2 2 2 3 3 4 4 4

8 8 8 9 9 9 10 10 10 9

13 13 13 13 14 14 14 14

17 17 17 18 18 18 18 18